this book belongs to:

_____

I am VERY important to God!

IT'S IMPORTANT.

written and
illustrated by
Joan Hutson

St. Paul Books & Media

Library of Congress Cataloging-in-Publication Data

Hutson, Joan.
    It's important / written and illustrated by Joan Hutson.
        p.   cm.
    Summary: Emphasizes the important things in life, such as not touching the
bird we love so much or not taking the cake before it is baked.
    ISBN 0-8198-3615-X
    [1. Conduct of life—Fiction. 2. Stories in rhyme.]   I. Title.
PZ8.3.H497It 1987
[E]—dc19   87-19397
                                                          CIP
                                                           AC

Printed in the U.S.A., by the Daughters of St. Paul
50 St. Paul's Ave., Boston, MA 02130

St. Paul Books & Media is the publishing house of the Daughters of St. Paul,
an international congregation of women religious serving the Church with the
communications media.

2 3 4 5 6 7 8 9   99 98 97 96 95 94 93 92

It's Important.

It's important

to be pondering
the ladybug's wandering...

8

It's important

to be quick
in a game of
  'rithmetic...

It's important

not to touch
when we love
the bird
so much...

It's important

to be flying
when the
March winds
are sighing...

14

It's important

not to take
the cake
before we bake...

It's important

to be winning
in the
very last inning...

It's most important

to see
when you like
the comedy...

It's important

to be still
hiding high
on a hill...

It's important

to be tending
while Mother
is mending...

It's important

to create
and then
appreciate...

It's important

to swing high
and try to
touch the sky...

It's important

to have a treat
in the blazing
summer heat...

It's important

to swim in the sea
and let the water
wave over me...

It's important

to be in camp
when the grass
all around
turns damp...

It's important

to be out wading
as soon as
the storm is fading...

It's important

to skip a rope
with a handful
of hope...

It's important

to be winning
with colored marbles
spinning...

It's important

to sing
a birthday song
with a cake
to go along...

It's important

to toss
the leaves about
when autumn is here
beyond a doubt...

It's important

to be sliding
down the
mountain-siding...

It's important

to have
Christmas Eve
to give as well
as to receive...

48

It's important

to love
and important
to be loved.

It's important

to pray
at the end
of the day.

Amen.

IT'S IMPORTANT

Joan Hutson

Joan Hutson is a woman of many talents. The mother of seven, she is also an author, artist, educator and musician.

Her books include: *The Wind Has Many Faces* (Abbey Press), *Heal My Heart, O Lord* (Ave Maria Press), *An Instrument of Your Peace* (Doubleday), *Hunger for Wholeness* (Ave Maria Press), *I Think I Know* (Ave Maria Press), *The Lord's Prayer* (Standard Publishing), *Love Never Ever Ends* (Standard Publishing), *Creation, Praise* (Harold Shaw Publishers), *Heaven and Earth* (Concordia Publishing House), *The Hail Mary* (St. Paul Books & Media), *It's Important* (St. Paul Books & Media), *My Happy Ones* (St. Paul Books & Media), *The Legend of the Nine Talents* (St. Paul Books & Media). She has also published approximately fifteen magazine articles.

She has illustrated many books, including most of her own, and there is a continuing exhibit of her paintings at Tri-County Hospital, in her hometown of Wadena, Minnesota.

As an educator, Mrs. Hutson has taught elementary school, high-school religion, and art and music classes for adults.

She is a liturgical guitarist and has been organist and choir director for her parish.

Bringing the message of God's love to His little ones is one of her specialties.

St. Paul Book & Media Centers

ALASKA
750 West 5th Ave., Anchorage, AK 99501 907-272-8183.
CALIFORNIA
3908 Sepulveda Blvd., Culver City, CA 90230 310-397-8676.
1570 Fifth Ave. (at Cedar Street), San Diego, CA 92101 619-232-1442; 619-232-1443.
46 Geary Street, San Francisco, CA 94108 415-781-5180.
FLORIDA
145 S.W. 107th Ave., Miami, FL 33174 305-559-6715; 305-559-6716.
HAWAII
1143 Bishop Street, Honolulu, HI 96813 808-521-2731.
ILLINOIS
172 North Michigan Ave., Chicago, IL 60601 312-346-4228; 312-346-3240.
LOUISIANA
4403 Veterans Memorial Blvd., Metairie, LA 70006 504-887-7631; 504-887-0113.
MASSACHUSETTS
50 St. Paul's Ave., Jamaica Plain, Boston, MA 02130 617-522-8911.
Rte. 1, 885 Providence Hwy., Dedham, MA 02026 617-326-5385.
MISSOURI
9804 Watson Rd., St. Louis, MO 63126 314-965-3512; 314-965-3571.
NEW JERSEY
561 U.S. Route 1, Wick Plaza, Edison, NJ 08817 908-572-1200.
NEW YORK
150 East 52nd Street, New York, NY 10022 212-754-1110.
78 Fort Place, Staten Island, NY 10301 718-447-5071; 718-447-5086.
OHIO
2105 Ontario Street (at Prospect Ave.), Cleveland, OH 44115 216-621-9427.
PENNSYLVANIA
214 W. DeKalb Pike, King of Prussia, PA 19406 215-337-1882; 215-337-2077.
SOUTH CAROLINA
243 King Street, Charleston, SC 29401 803-577-0175.
TEXAS
114 Main Plaza, San Antonio, TX 78205 512-224-8101.
VIRGINIA
1025 King Street, Alexandria, VA 22314 703-549-3806.
CANADA
3022 Dufferin Street, Toronto, Ontario, Canada M6B 3T5 416-781-9131.